T0197388

This book is dedicated to my beloved
and brilliant daughter Eva Ceylan.
Sibel Ordek

The illustrations in this book are dedicated to my beloved, amazing son Arman Sahin.
Evin Ozalp Sahin

To order additional copies of this book, contact:
Xlibris
UK TFN: 0800 0148620 (Toll Free inside the UK)
UK Local: 02036 956328 (+44 20 3695 6328 from outside the UK)
www.xlibrispublishing.co.uk
Orders@ Xlibrispublishing.co.uk

ISBN: 978-1-6641-1463-0 (sc)
ISBN: 978-1-6641-1462-3 (e)

Print information available on the last page

Rev. date: 02/10/2021

The Great Tree and The Goldfinches

STORY BY

Sibel Ordek

ILLUSTRATED BY

Evin Ozalp Sahin

Chapter 1: The Goodness Land

I t was a lovely day. The Sun was shining gloriously; there was a refreshing, gentle breeze, and the sky was bright blue. You could see a couple of cotton-like clouds gliding casually. They looked as though they were enjoying the sun and dancing in the soft blowing wind.

Pearl and Zipper, a pair of goldfinches, were flying high up in the sky on this gorgeous day. Their unique red faces were stunning, as were the white patches behind their eyes and their black scruffs and domes. They also had yellow wing patches, black tails, and long-pointed beaks.

They were journeying to find the Great Tree in Goodness Land, where they could build their nest. It would be a nest to welcome the new members of their family. They had been dreaming of the Great Tree since childhood because their grandparents used to tell stories about it.

According to Pearl's grandparents, the spectacular Great Tree had been standing alone for centuries in Anatolia; a faraway land that had been home to many different cultures. It stood secluded in Goodness Land on the top of a hill with a waterfall on its side. It was a giant, living miracle that had earned a reputation for providing excellent shelter to those who needed it. Unbelievably green, during all four seasons; Its leaves never fell, even in the winter. So, the inhabitants of Goodness Land could have shelter whenever they needed it. The tree would quickly expand so that no one was left outside. Some say that it, once, accommodated a rhino. It was always warm beneath the Great Tree, as it wouldn't let adverse weather such as strong wind, snow or rain disturb its inhabitants. Therefore, they were never cold.

The Great Tree bore fruit all year round, and not only the inhabitants but all the creatures passing by could get food whenever they needed. The fruit was of many

different types such as bananas, apples, oranges, cherries, apricots, figs, and even included almonds, pecan, walnuts, not to mention olives. Stunningly beautiful flowers grew all around the tree. Dandelions, orchids, golden daisies, rainbow rose, sunflowers, sedums, wild lilacs and jade plants. There was even a beehive in it. Grandma assured Pearl that the bees were peaceful, sociable and very friendly. The flowers provided nectar and pollen for them so that they could make honey.

Her grandparents lived there after her Grandpa had wounded his wing. They needed shelter. The Great Tree warmly welcomed them, and they even made a special potion with its leaves and resin that healed grandpa's wound. They had a nest on it. They also had their first nestlings there and stayed until they learned how to fly. The Great Tree named the new-borns. It was a tradition that had been carried out for centuries. Grandma used to say that it was the best place to lay eggs. The moment young Pearl heard that; she knew that she had to have her nestlings there too.

7

It was their time to have their own family, so they were on their way. Pearl felt that it was taking ages, but it was only a couple of weeks since they had started their journey to find The Great Tree in The Goodness Land.

During their journey, they passed over so many spectacular woodlands sitting between hills and high mountains.

The woodlands were full of impressive trees that could provide a home for them.

They saw every possible shade of green in the trees and the grass. There were multi-coloured flowers all around, and flowing rivers filled with happy creatures. There were small and pleasant waterfalls.

The sun was shining brightly over the trees, but none of them felt right for Pearl and Zipper. They were not The Great Tree that they had been searching for. So, they didn't want to settle in these lands, even though their search had been fruitless for the past few weeks.

Chapter 2: We Will Conquer

Pearl and Zipper were exhausted and in despair. Their small wings were growing weak as they had been flapping for hours.

Pearl saw a tree where they could rest, and she swooped down to it without warning. Zipper was baffled when he saw her landing on the tree, yet he followed her. Pearl looked at her husband with love in her eyes, trying to smile, and explained, "I was worn out and needed a break." She seemed like she was about to dissolve into tears.

"That's okay, my dear. Let's get a bit of rest," responded Zipper, and kissed her.

With that sweet kiss, she was beaming with joy. Almost unbelievably, she got her energy back. They loved each other so much that a small smooch and a smile could make them happy in the twinkling of an eye.

"What about some delicious dandelions or scrumptious thistles?" asked Zipper. Pearl smiled and nodded.

Off they went to get some food. While they were enjoying their lunch, the gentle breeze became a storm with thunder and lightning. The sky wasn't bright blue anymore. It had changed in a flash.

Pearl looked up to the sky and gulped, "Look at the dark clouds up there! I think it is going to rain."

"Come on, we need to find shelter quickly before it starts pouring down," Zipper said.

They found a spot in-between the big rocks and got in quickly. It was darker than outside, but at least they wouldn't be soaked. It rained all afternoon and all night. They fell fast asleep.

Pearl dreamt of her Grandpa that night. He was saying, "My dear Pearl, the power and the strength you need is within you. Please never lose your faith, never give up, stay motivated and keep moving forward, and I promise you will conquer."

"We will conquer grandpa," chirped Pearl in her dream.

In the morning, they had their breakfast. There was no more rain, and they set off without delay.

Chapter 3: I Can Feel It

As they were high up in the sky, flapping, Pearl started singing a song;

I can feel it.

Today is the day.

Every ounce of strength

Will take us to it.

Closer and closer

To the Great Tree.

Every ounce of strength

Will take us to it.

Closer and closer

To the Great Tree.

I can feel it.

Today is the day.

They flapped and flapped and flapped and flapped. These tiny birds were very persistent, refusing to give up or let go, despite their tiredness and their weak wings. They wouldn't stop flapping until they found their home, the Great Tree.

"My grandma told me that we would know once we found it. It's not something that

we could overlook," said Pearl and added, "I understand what she means by that now...,
LOOK Zipper, **LOOK**!"

Zipper gaped at the sight in astonishment for a second. "**WOW**! I was not expecting this!" he exclaimed in surprise.

"It is awe-inspiring, isn't it?" asked Pearl.

"It is indeed," responded Zipper.

They had seen nothing like it before in their lives. It was beyond their imagination.

Finally, their endless determination, persistence and faith had paid off.

Pearl, overjoyed, sang a song again and Zipper joined in too.

I knew it was the day.

I knew it would be tall and green.

But it is;

Taller than we thought.

Greener than we thought.

It is a joy to our eyes.

It is unique.

It is peaceful and refreshing.

We found the perfect place.

We found our home.

"Welcome," greeted the Great Tree warmly.

"Thank you," they replied, excited.

"Please allow me to say that your pleasant voices and wondrous song has gone through me. You are gifted," complimented The Great Tree and added, smiling, "You seem contented."

"Yes, we are. We have been looking for you for some time and to be honest with you, it wasn't an easy journey," explained Zipper.

"We have been listening to stories about The Goodness Land and you, Great Tree, since our childhood and we, particularly myself, have been fond of you ever since," explained Pearl shyly.

"Don't be shy my child," encouraged The Great Tree. "I am honoured. Come on, tell me about your plans, please. What do you want to do?"

"We want to make our nest here and have our nestlings as my grandparents did," said Pearl, asking permission by adding "of course if you don't mind."

"I don't mind at all, and I'd be delighted to have you," answered the Great Tree.

"That's very kind of you. We really appreciate it," Pearl and Zipper replied together.

"Go ahead and explore, choose the branch that you want your nest on," said the Great Tree, smiling.

Chapter 4: Building the Nest

Pearl and Zipper happily started wheeling around the tree. They were seeking the best branch for their nest. The Great Tree had a hard, large and thick trunk. From that thick trunk grew numerous branches that reached to the sky, some even to the clouds. The views from the top were magnificent.

"It was a long journey, even frustrating at times; but I am glad that we never gave up. It was worth our effort!" said Pearl.

"You are dead right!" agreed Zipper.

The Great Tree had endless possibilities. Therefore, it took quite a while, for them to decide. Whenever they thought, "Yes, this is the perfect spot," they saw a better place, and that happened again, and again.

They finally agreed on a spot located quite high in the nooks of tree's branches. It was sheltered from the rain, wind, and predators so that Pearl could comfortably lay her eggs.

That evening they were relaxed and happy. They were where they wanted to be and already knew where to build the nest.

The next morning, Zipper started looking for materials: Leaves, grass, moss and twigs and even hair and wool. He thought that Pearl would use them to bind the nest together.

Zipper was quite picky about the materials. Like most proud fathers, he wanted the best for his family. He chose the best of the best and started carrying them up to the tree so that Pearl could build the nest neatly.

While Zipper was choosing materials, Pearl was thinking about how to build the nest and where to start.

Once Zipper brought the materials, Pearl took over and started building the nest. She was enthusiastic but something was wrong, and she couldn't work out what it was.

She was having difficulty staying focused.

"It requires a great deal of close attention, and I can't concentrate on it!" exclaimed Pearl.

Zipper saw her struggle. She needed to take it easy. So, he stepped in and sang a song to calm her down.

My gorgeous wife;
You are the one I love.
You are the best
Nest builder
I know, Oh I know
You will be the best
Mum ever.
All you need
Is to take it easy.
Don't give up;
You are the one I love.

They had a break that afternoon, enjoying the surroundings and the fresh air, and even played hide and seek. They had so much fun that they were soon relaxed. They put their feet up that evening and had a good night's sleep.

Pearl awoke early in the morning as she wanted to restart building the nest with the first light. Zipper was awake early, too. He went to find more materials should there be any need.

It wasn't an easy job; it was necessary to be careful and diligent. That's why Pearl considered everything; every twig used was sifted through before using it in the nest. She worked like an engineer; designed and then constructed. She weaved the nest so tightly with twigs, used some wool and hair to bind it. It took about a week to build it. She flapped above, looked at her creation, and smiled. She was satisfied; because they had made what they wanted, what they needed — their home.

"One more thing," she thought and then she put in the last touch by lining it with leaves and grass. "A soft bed for the nestlings," she whispered, smiling.

Chapter 5: Laying the Eggs

Zipper and Pearl had a quiet night in their nest, enjoying the beauty of the moonlight as they snuggled up with smile on their beaks.

They got up with the first light of the sun, feeling rested.

"It is time for laying the eggs. I will be able to lay one egg each morning," said Pearl.

"Really? Oh Great! I can't wait for my children!" yelled Zipper excitedly.

Pearl smiled nervously and asked, "What day is it?"

"It's Monday," Zipper responded.

"I was born on a Monday too," said Pearl, smiling, as she settled down, took a deep breath, and started laying the eggs.

She laid the first one that morning and sat on it all day long.

The second one came on Tuesday morning, and she sat on both all day long.

On Wednesday morning, the third one came, and she sat on all three of them all day long.

The fourth one came on Thursday morning she sat on all four of them all day long.

The fifth one came on Friday morning

she sat on all of them all day long.

Zipper, in the meantime, carried food and water for Pearl as she had to keep the eggs warm.

"That's all," said Pearl, smiling joyfully. She was relieved. A couple of happy tears fell from her eyes. She was proud of what she had achieved.

Zipper was over the moon. "I am a father of five! I am a father of five!" He was moving his wings up and down with excitement.

Pearl continuously sat on the eggs on Saturday and Sunday too.

Later, Zipper took a turn and sat on the eggs, letting Pearl rest as she had backache.

Both, Pearl and Zipper, sat on the eggs for about 15 days, taking turns to keep them warm.

All that time they sang lullabies to their babies, telling them how difficult it had been to find the perfect place for their family, how much their parents loved them, how beautiful their nest was, how magical the surroundings were, and how lucky they all were.

One morning, Pearl and Zipper went out together to get some food for the nestlings as they were about to hatch. They were sure that they would be back before they hatched.

Pearl looked at to the Great Tree and asked, "Please look after the eggs. I don't want any predators to take them away. We will go and get some food for them. I trust you will keep them safe."

"I promise I will keep them safe," the Great Tree reassured.

"I am sure you will," said Pearl, and off they went.

In the meantime, Snore, a snake who was hungry and looking for food, heard the conversation between Pearl and The Great Tree. He smiled with a hiss and said to himself, "I have found my dinner."

Snore slithered up to the Great Tree.

The Great Tree felt him and kept an eye on him, as she wasn't sure what he wanted.

"Hey Snore, what's up?" asked The Great Tree.

"I'm fine. Just looking for a quiet spot to rest if you don't mind," replied Snore.

"Of course, no problem. Please try to keep quiet," replied The Great Tree, knowing that it was impossible as everybody in Goodness Land was fed up with his snoring. That's why they called him Snore.

Snore continued slithering higher and higher.

The Great Tree started getting suspicious as Snore usually wouldn't climb so high. He had a fear of heights. That's why she asked, "Isn't it high for you?"

"Oh, don't worry about me, I am trying to overcome my fear" explained Snore to the Great Tree. "I am a little bit hungry though, and I will get the eggs," thought Snore in his mind.

But Snore was not aware that The Great Tree understood his evil purpose and would not allow him to get the eggs. He had promised Pearl, and he was keen to keep that promise. He never broke a promise. He covered the nest with his leaves and protected it with his branches.

Then the Great Tree started shaking some of his lower branches to shake some of the leaves down onto Snore's face, to disturb him. He was hoping to stop him.

But it didn't stop Snore. He continued slithering up.

Then the Great Tree waggled the branch that Snore was on and made him fall onto the lower limbs.

"Hey, what's wrong with you?" asked Snore hissing angrily. He continued slithering up as he was starving.

The Great Tree was getting furious. "I know what you are trying to do Snore; I will not let you get the eggs. You can't reach them!"

"Oh, I can, and I will. You can't stop me!" Snore jumped to a branch. He was falling but caught it with his tail in the last second. He recovered and quickly slithered up.

"You know Snore; you are wasting your time. I will not let you get the eggs," warned The Great Tree.

The Great Tree was aware that it was going to be quite difficult to catch him. Snore was moving with high speed, continuously jumping and slithering from one branch to another. He was getting closer to the nest.

The Great Tree didn't want to hurt Snore, but he couldn't let that naughty snake get the eggs either.

He had lost his patience; it was time to show the snake who was the boss!

Thinking quickly and cleverly, he caught Snore by his tail with one of his branches.

He swung him about and threw him to another branch and onto another one and another.

He continued doing this until Snore got dizzy.

Then he hurled Snore away, far away from the eggs, to the other side of the waterfall. Snore hated being soaking wet, and he didn't dare get into the water.

"YOU, **SILLY**, **NAUGHTY SNAKE**, do not come near me ever again!" shouted The Great Tree.

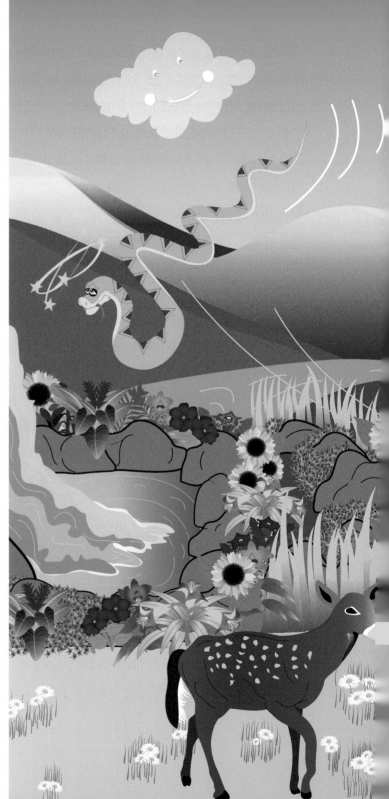

Chapter 7: Nestlings and The Great Tree

The first egg cracked. The nestling was impatiently trying to cut through the shell. She was tiny and had no feathers. She raised her head on her wobbly neck, attempting to open her eyes and was dazzled by the bright daylight.

While the first nestling was struggling to emerge from eggshell, she rolled to the side and bumped into the next one, causing the second egg to crack.

The first nestling was a bit nervous. She opened her eyes and, once she got used to the daylight looked around. "I hope I have a big family," she thought to herself. She wanted to meet the other family members. Instead, she saw some leaves, grasses, and four other eggs.

Spotting her, The Great Tree said: "Hey there... you... young lady."

"Hello," The nestling replied, with a cracked voice. "Are you my family?" she asked hopefully.

"You could say that," answered The Great Tree and continued, "Don't worry. This is your home. You are safe here. I am The Great Tree. Your nest is on one of my branches. Your parents went to get some food for you, and they will be here any minute."

"Thank you," replied the nestling, reassured.

In the meantime, the second nestling started cutting through the shell. After a while, another beak emerged from the eggshell.

The third one and the fourth one followed him. All four nestlings were out, but the fifth one was still, there was no movement.

One of the nestlings said to her sister, "Come on, I know you can do it. Pecking the shell will break it, and you can come out as we did."

The nestling inside heard her sister, but she was weak and scared. It was pitch-dark.

Her siblings wanted to help her. One of them started pecking the eggshell from the outside, even though it was difficult standing on his wobbly legs. Seeing this, the others joined him.

All four of them were pecking the egg as they wanted their sibling to come out and join them. Then the one inside gathered her strength with her siblings' encouragement and started pecking at the shell.

Working together, they cracked the eggshell in no time, and the fifth one's beak emerged.

This time the siblings chirped with pleasure, saying "You did it! We did it!" to their sister.

"That's it!" whooped the Great Tree, "You did a great job, well done. The best teamwork ever! I know you all are a bit cold as you don't have any feathers yet. Let me cover you with my leaves until your parents are back."

"You are the best!" screamed the nestlings.

"May I name you all, please? I am sure your parents would like to name you but, it is a tradition that I name the new-borns here. If you don't want them to be your

first names, you can use them as nicknames, " offered The Great Tree.

"It is okay, I guess," said one of them.

"I am happy that you gave me the green light," said the Great Tree and continued;

"Hmm, let me see... you, the first arrival. You are brave. That's why I want to call you *Berna*, which means 'young and brave' in Turkish."

"You are very generous and supportive. That's why I want to call you *Albert*, which means "noble" in German".

"You, to my amazement, you were born with your book and glasses. That's why I want to call you *Bookworm*, which means 'one who is fond of reading' in English.

"You, young lady, you are such a beauty. That's why I want to call you *Rose*. It is a delicate flower, like yourself."

"Last but not least, you are the bravest of them all, a fighter. That's why I want to call you *Imelda*, which means 'powerful fighter' in Spanish."

"Well, do you like your names?" asked The Great Tree.

"We love them!" cried the nestlings and they added, "You are wonderful."

"How many languages do you know?" asked Imelda.

"I can speak most of the languages spoken in the world. I had so many visitors from all around the world and learned their languages," answered the Great Tree.

"Really!" shouted Albert, Berna and Rose at once.

"You are so talented!" exclaimed Bookworm, eagerly adding "I want to meet all your visitors, read all of the books and learn all the languages too."

"I have no doubt that you will!" The Great Tree said with a smile.

At that moment, Pearl and Zipper came back and happily hugged the nestlings.

The nestlings introduced themselves to their parents by their given names.

"I have a German name, it is *Albert*," pronounced the first nestling.

"I am called *Berna* as I am brave," said the second, proudly.

"I am *Bookworm*," said the third showing his book and touching the frame of his glasses'.

"My name is *Rose*," said the fourth nestling gently.

"I am a powerful fighter, *Imelda*," said the fifth, trying to pose proudly on her wobbly legs.

"What beautiful names you all have!" bubbled Pearl.

"Meaningful and, spot on!" asserted Zipper.

"I am a bit hungry, mum. Can I please have some food?" asked Rose politely.

"Me too, me too!" exclaimed the others.

"I am not surprised." smiled Pearl and started feeding them sunflower seeds.

The parents said, "We can't thank you enough for looking after our babies." to the Great Tree.

"My pleasure," replied the Great Tree.

Never give up and I promise you will **CONQUER!**

ABOUT THE AUTHOR

SIBEL ORDEK is the author behind "The Great Tree and The Goldfinches". She studied International Logistics, worked in corporations for many years. She developed a passion for short stories during her career and pursued her passion for writing. Here she is with her first book; "The Great Tree and The Goldfinches".

She is a mother, a daughter, a sister, a friend to many and an aunt. She loves nature and animals. She lives in the United Kingdom with her daughter, Eva Ceylan and their beloved dog, Laddie-Cosmo.

Printed in the United States
by Baker & Taylor Publisher Services